PEACHTREE

PEACHTREE

# A Clever Beatrice Christmas

## Author's Note

Many of the Christmas traditions of Beatrice's far north were a celebration of the wintry out-doors—choosing and decorating the Christmas tree, making a cake (called *Bûche de Noël*) that looked like a log from the woodpile, winding through a snowy village on Christmas Eve. Père Noël, the French-Canadian version of Santa Claus, has a special fondness for children like Beatrice—little ones clever enough to convince others to believe.

*For my mother, Queen of Christmas*
—M. W.

*To my dad*
—H. M. S.

Atheneum Books for Young Readers
An imprint of Simon & Schuster Children's Publishing Division
1230 Avenue of the Americas
New York, New York 10020
Text copyright © 2006 by Margaret Willey
Illustrations copyright © 2006 by Heather M. Solomon
All rights reserved, including the right of
reproduction in whole or in part in any form.
Book design by Sonia Chaghatzbanian
The text for this book is set in Goudy.
The illustrations for this book were rendered
in watercolor, collage, acrylic, and oil paint.
Manufactured in China
First Edition
1 2 3 4 5 6 7 8 9 10

Library of Congress Cataloging-in-Publication Data
Willey, Margaret.
A Clever Beatrice Christmas / Margaret Willey ; illustrated by
Heather M. Solomon.—1st ed.
p. cm.
Summary: As Christmas approaches, Clever Beatrice sets out
to prove the existence of Père Noël to three questioning children.
ISBN-13: 978-0-689-87017-0
ISBN-10: 0-689-87017-5
1. Santa Claus—Juvenile fiction. [1. Santa Claus—Fiction.
2. Christmas—Fiction.]
I. Solomon, Heather, ill. II. Title.
PZ7.W65548Cle 2006
[E]—dc22
2005010281

# A Clever Beatrice Christmas

by Margaret Willey    illustrated by Heather M. Solomon

Atheneum Books for Young Readers
New York   London   Toronto   Sydney

Christmas was coming to the far north, and Beatrice and her mother hurried to the village store, pulling an empty sled. They needed flour and sugar and cocoa to make a special Christmas cake—the *Bûche de Noël*. As they came to the frozen river, Beatrice saw three children skating. The littlest one, a girl, waved and called, "Are you the one they call Clever Beatrice?"

"I am!" Beatrice called back. "I live up the hill with my mother."

"We have heard of you!" cried the taller of two boys. "Come and skate with us! We have many questions to ask you!"

While Beatrice's mother went on with her sled to the village, Beatrice made her way carefully down the riverbank to the edge of the ice.

The taller boy skated over in fine skates with curling loops at the tip of each blade. "I am Rollo and this is my brother, René," he said. "Antoinette is our cousin. Our fathers have come from Montreal to work at the lumber camp. Let us pull you along on the ice. It is perfect today!"

The boys each took a hand and pulled Beatrice while Antoinette skated in a circle around them. "We three have many questions to ask you about Père Noël!" Antoinette said.

"Oh, I know all about Père Noël!" Beatrice said. "He is coming very soon."

"But can you tell us how Père Noël can bring presents to so many children in one night?" asked René.

"He travels on the wind all the way from the North Pole in a sleigh pulled by many reindeer," Beatrice told them. "In the back of the sleigh is the great sack of toys he brings so that every girl and boy will find a special present on Christmas morning."

"Have you yourself ever seen Père Noël?" Antoinette asked.

"He comes after midnight," Beatrice explained, "when children are snug in their beds. But late in the night I have sometimes heard the ringing of the bells on his sleigh!"

Rollo skated away to think about this. When he came back he said, "There are many sleighs in the village with bells on them that travel at night, yes? Couldn't you have heard one of them and thought it was Père Noël's?"

"Oh, but I am quite sure it was Père Noël's!" Beatrice insisted.

"How could you be sure?" asked René.

Beatrice thought a moment, and then announced, "On Christmas Day I will bring you a bell from Père Noël's very own sleigh!"

The three skaters gasped with delight.

Just then Beatrice's mother appeared on the road, returning from the store with the sled piled high. "Ask your new friends if they would like to help us make the *Bûche de Noël*!" she called. The children cried, *"Oui!"* and followed Beatrice home.

In the kitchen, Beatrice's friends helped make a long flat cake in a pan. When the cake had cooled, they spread the top of it with sweet cream and jelly, then rolled it into a log, which they covered all over with chocolate frosting. Beatrice scored the frosting with a fork to make it look like rough bark, and her friends made little frosting mushrooms. It looked so much like a real log that Beatrice's mother said she would have to be careful not to throw it in the fireplace in the morning.

The next day was even closer to Christmas, and Beatrice's mother woke Beatrice early. "Come have your breakfast, my girl. This morning we must find our Christmas tree."

Beatrice ate her porridge quickly and put on her boots. They walked down the hill to a patch of young firs, where Beatrice helped her mother cut down a small tree and fasten it to their sled with rope. As they were walking back, Beatrice heard children calling her name through the trees—it was Rollo and René and Antoinette, all wearing furry hats.

Beatrice's mother took the tree inside so that the children could sled down Beatrice's hill.

At the bottom Antoinette said, "Beatrice, we three have been wondering and wondering how Père Noël stays warm all through the night on Christmas Eve."

"I have heard that he wears a special cape," Beatrice told her friends. "A beautiful cape with shiny buttons. It falls clear to the ground and keeps him as warm as a sleeping bear!"

Rollo thought about this as they trudged back up the hill. "But Monsieur Le Pain has a very heavy winter cape, and still he hurries to deliver all his bread before sundown," he pointed out. "And Charlie Running Wolf has a cape made from the fur of a real bear, but he says that in winter it is sometimes too cold for him to leave his lodge. So how can Père Noël have a cape that keeps him warm enough to be in the north wind all night long?"

Beatrice thought a moment, and then announced, "On Christmas Day I will bring you a button from Père Noël's very own cape!"

The three friends clapped their hands at the very idea.

Just then Beatrice heard her mother calling: "Come, petites, help decorate the Christmas tree!"

The children strung popcorn and pine-cone garlands and wound them round the little tree, along with sprigs of winterberry and holly. Beatrice made a star out of paper and lifted up little Antoinette to put it on the top of the tree.

Then Beatrice's mother brought out their Christmas crèche, which had long ago belonged to Beatrice's great-grandmother Ondine from Normandy. The children arranged the figures—Joseph and Mary, three wise men from the east, a shepherd carrying a lamb, an angel, a donkey, a goat, and a sheep. The last figure was the infant Jesus in a manger.

Then it was Christmas Eve!

In Beatrice's village many people gathered on Christmas Eve for a great feast in the center of the town. Beatrice and her mother brought *tourtieres*, and Rollo and René's mother brought a rum cake, and Antoinette's father brought a whole smoked goose. There was a long wooden table heaped with food! The celebrating continued until nearly midnight, when the villagers traveled in a line to the church for midnight mass, holding candles and singing carols as they walked under the stars.

Rollo and René walked close behind Beatrice, and Antoinette walked between Beatrice and her mother, holding Beatrice's hand. Rollo whispered in Beatrice's ear, "How will you be sure that the man in the sleigh wearing the cape is truly Père Noël?"

"I have heard that Père Noël has the brightest, clearest blue eyes in the far north," Beatrice whispered back. "And a beautiful snow-white beard, so very soft that it is more like a cloud than a beard!"

Rollo walked farther, thinking about this. Then he said, "But Herr Herman the Finlander has a white beard, and Monsieur Tremblay at the village store has a very nice beard too! Wouldn't it be easy to see one of these men in the darkness and think it was Père Noël?"

Beatrice thought for a moment, and then announced, "On Christmas Day I will bring you a curl from Père Noël's very own beard!"

The children were so excited to hear this that they could barely sit still during midnight mass. Afterward Monsieur Le Pain took Beatrice and her mother home in his wagon.

He gave Beatrice's mother a brioche tied with a red ribbon, and she gave him a plate of sugar tarts and wished him *Joyeux Noël*. "Now hurry into your nightgown, my girl," she said to Beatrice, "and I will put out the *Bûche de Noël*."

She tucked Beatrice in, but Beatrice did not fall asleep. Instead she wiggled her feet and pinched her arms and counted to one hundred. Finally she heard the sound of bells coming closer and closer, until they stopped outside of her house. She looked out her window and saw many reindeer, then heard the sound of heavy boots crunching the snow. Quick as a mouse she put on her boots, grabbed a pair of scissors, and hurried to the door.

There stood an old man in a long cape with a snow-white beard and the brightest blue eyes she had ever seen. Over one shoulder, he carried a huge sack bulging with toys.

"You are supposed to be snug in your bed, little Beatrice!" he said.

"I was quite snug in my bed only a moment ago," Beatrice told him, "but then I heard that one of the bells on your sleigh was not ringing properly. It bothered me so much that I just had to get up and tell you."

"Is that so?" asked Père Noël with a laugh.

"Don't worry, I will take care of it for you!" Beatrice said, and she ran outside and quickly cut off one little bell from the side of the sleigh and put it in the pocket of her nightgown.

When she came back inside she asked, "Is your cape really as warm as the fur of a bear, Père Noël?"

"It is, indeed," said Père Noël, patting where the cape covered his belly.

"I am only asking because I see that one of the buttons is loose and may fall off in the wind and hit one of your reindeer on the nose!"

"Is that so?" asked Père Noël, laughing again.

"Don't worry, I will take care of it for you!" said Beatrice, and with her scissors she snipped off one button and slipped it into her pocket.

Then she looked up at Père Noël's beard. "Now that I am seeing you up close, Père Noël, I find that your beard is a little crooked on one side."

"Is that so?" asked Père Noël, stroking his beard.

"Don't worry, I will take care of it for you!" said Beatrice. She motioned for Père Noël to lean closer and cut off one curl—soft as a cloud—and quickly put it into her pocket.

"And now will you tell your new friends that you have seen me, little clever one?" asked Père Noël.

Beatrice's eyes grew wide with surprise. "I will," she said. "And I will tell them that you are the cleverest of all."

Père Noël cut a huge piece of the *Bûche de Noël* for the long ride back to the North Pole. "And now you really must go to bed," he said, "for I have something special in my sack that you must not see until morning." He put his warm hand against Beatrice's cheek, and before she knew it, she was back in her own bed, fast asleep.

In the morning she awoke and found in her pocket the bell, the button, and the wisp of beard. "Oh, Mother," she cried, sitting up in her bed, "I must go to the village at once to see my friends!"

Her mother laughed. "Your friends can wait, my girl. Right now you must come see what Père Noël has left for you under the tree!" She led Beatrice from her bed by the hand.

Beatrice saw that Père Noël had left her a pair of new skates with shiny blades. But that was not all! Inside one of the skates, curled into a ball, was a kitten with bright blue eyes, a bell at its collar, and fur as white and soft as the beard of Père Noël!

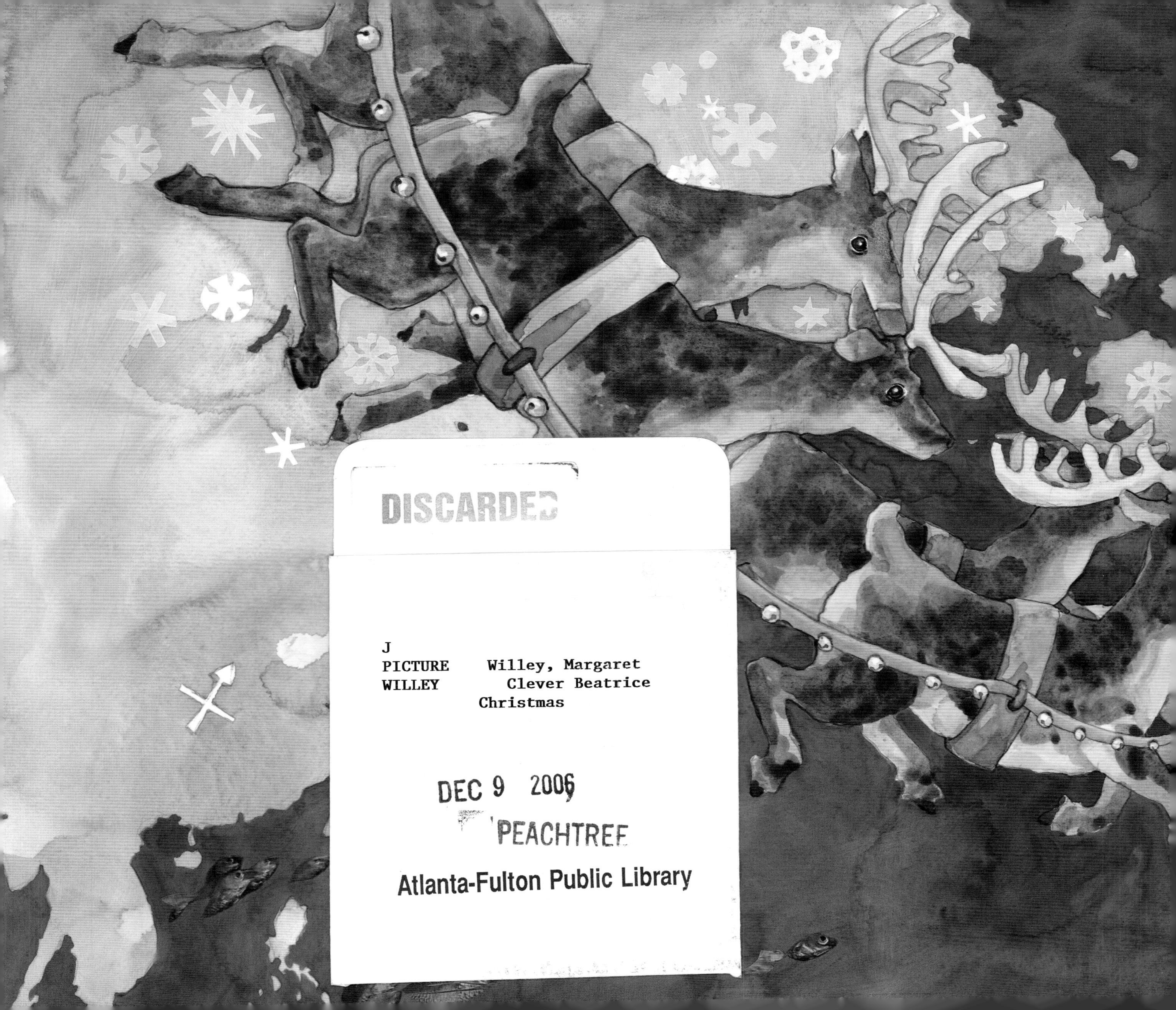